Bright
Summaries.com

The Girl and the Night

BY GUILLAUME MUSSO

The Girl and the Night

BY GUILLAUME MUSSO

GUILLAUME MUSSO

FRENCH WRITER

- **Born in 1974 in Antibes (France).**
- **Some of his works:**
  - *And then...* (2004), novel.
  - *The Angel's Call* (2011), novel.
  - *Central Park* (2014), novel.

It was at the age of thirty, in 2001, that the Frenchman Guillaume Musso published his first novel. However, he only met with real success three years later, with *Et après...* which was adapted for the cinema in 2008. Since 2004, Musso has been publishing novels at the rate of one per year. French readers respond to each publication. In 2012, he was awarded the Chevalier de l'Ordre des Arts et des Lettres. In 2017, he sold more than one and a half million copies of his books, making him the most widely read author in France for the seventh consecutive year.

Musso is fascinated by the United States, where most of his novels are set. His novels are best known for combining a love story with a fast-paced investigation. Since 2011 and *L'Appel de l'ange*, his writing has become more of a thriller, which has earned him the nickname "the king of suspense" by French journalist and writer Bernard Thomasson.

THE GIRL AND THE NIGHT

A BREATHTAKING THRILLER

- **Genre**: crime novel

- **Reference edition**: *La Jeune Fille et la nuit*, Paris, Calmann Levy, 2018, 424 p.

- **1st edition**: 2018

- **Themes**: friendship, love, family, murder, revenge, lies

For Thomas Degalais, the 50th anniversary ceremony of his old high school turns into a nightmare. Twenty-five years earlier, with the help of his friend Maxime, he buried a corpse in the wall of the gym. This same gym is about to be demolished, and their secret could be revealed at any moment...

With *La Jeune Fille et la nuit*, Musso has truly anchored himself in the genre of crime fiction. Right up to the last page, the dramas and skilfully constructed plot twists multiply, keeping the reader on the edge of his seat. This is evidenced by the popular success that the novel was in the summer of 2018: over 500,000 copies were sold in France between April and August 2018.

This change of literary direction corresponds to a desire on the part of the author to "get out of his comfort zone". It is also his first novel for Calmann-Lévy, after leaving his publisher XO Éditions.

SUMMARY

A TERRIBLE SECRET

Spring 2017. Thomas Degalais returns to his hometown in the south of France to attend the 50th anniversary ceremony of his high school. On this occasion, the gymnasium will be demolished and replaced by a new building, financed by mysterious investors. Thomas is worried because the gym is hiding a secret that he concealed 25 years ago...

Thomas is sitting at a café when a stranger shoves him, splashing his trousers. When he returns from the bathroom, the newspaper he was reading has the word "revenge" crossed out and a pair of sunglasses with it, identical to those owned by Vinca, the girl he fell in love with as a teenager and who disappeared 25 years earlier. No one knows what happened to her, but many believe that she ran away with her philosophy teacher, with whom she was rumoured to be having an affair.

The next day, a cocktail party is organised for the former students. Worried that his secret will be revealed, Thomas goes to the party and meets up with some of his classmates: Fanny, his former girlfriend who loves photography; Maxime, who used to live next door to him; and Stéphane Pianelli, a journalist at Nice-Matin. The latter tells him that a month earlier, following floods in the school's cellar, a surprising discovery was made: an old locker, put away for twenty years, contained 100,000 francs hidden in a leather bag where Vinca's fingerprints were found. For Stéphane, this discovery proves that Vinca did not run away (otherwise she would have taken the money with her), but that she was killed by her lover.

Thomas shows Maxime the newspaper and the glasses. His friend admits that he has also received threats. The two men share a terrible secret: in December 1992, when they were high school students, they killed a man and buried his body in the wall of the gymnasium under construction.

A flashback reveals the circumstances of the murder. In 1992, Thomas, who had stayed at the boarding school to revise, discovers inflammatory letters in a book belonging to Vinca. They are signed by "Alexis", the name of the attractive 27-year-old philosophy teacher. The letters confirm the rumour and drive him mad with grief. His friend then calls him and asks to see him, as she is not feeling well; "cursing [his] weakness, [his] lack of self-esteem" (p. 92), Thomas goes to the girl's room. Vinca, very weak and feverish, is lying in bed. She confesses that she is pregnant and that Alexis has forced her to have sex.

Blinded by rage, Thomas entrusts Vinca to his friend Fanny before going to the professor's flats, armed with an iron bar. "Trapped in a spiral" (p. 99), the young man attacks Alexis. After a moment's hesitation on the part of his assailant, the professor tries to defend himself.

Maxime then arrives, armed with a knife, and delivers the fatal blow. The two young men are shocked and do not know what to do. Maxime then decides to tell his father, Francis, a construction worker, who was present at the school on the site of the new gymnasium, with his colleague Ahmed. To protect his son and his friend, Francis decides to bury the body in the wall of the gym under construction.

DISTURBING REVELATIONS

With the gym about to be demolished, their secret will be discovered. While Francis and Ahmed are now dead (from a burglary gone wrong and a long illness, respectively), Maxime and Thomas are at risk. To protect Maxime and his family life, Thomas is ready to take full responsibility for the crime. Both men are convinced that someone else knows what happened on that fateful day in December 1992, but they don't know who it is.

The day after the murder, Thomas had already wanted to confess, but had changed his mind to protect his accomplices. At the school, everyone seemed to believe that Alexis had run off with Vinca, including the police. Indeed, testimonies concur: a young redheaded girl, matching Vinca's description, was seen on a train to Paris and then in a hotel with a man resembling Alexis. This runaway love affair then became the official version. But Thomas, who of course knows the truth, thinks that Vinca has run away with someone else. Torn by guilt, he wants to know if Vinca's disappearance the day after Alexis' murder is linked to it and if he is responsible.

The first step in his investigation takes him to the high school library, where he seeks out *The Girl and Death*, a book written fifteen years earlier by Stéphane Piannelli, who had already investigated the disappearance without making any significant discoveries. Convinced that Stéphane can help him, Thomas offers to work with him to solve Vinca's disappearance.

On his way back to his car, Thomas discovers an anonymous envelope on the windscreen. It contains photographs of his father, Richard Degalais, the former school headmaster, kissing Vinca. Knowing Fanny's passion for photography, Thomas has the intuition that his former friend is the author of the pictures. The young woman confesses that she took them to discredit Vinca in Thomas's eyes, because she was in love with him. She also informs his friend that she has also received threatening letters, as she knows about the presence of a corpse in the wall of the gym, Ahmed having confessed the crime to her shortly before his death. Thomas then confronts his father, as he believes he is involved in Vinca's disappearance. But Richard denies it: he only confesses that he gave the money to the girl because she was blackmailing him.

Thomas then returns to the school and finds the book he discovered twenty-five years earlier, which contained Alexis' love letters to Vinca. He realises that the handwriting is not the same as the one on his philosophy course papers, annotated by Alexis. He realises that Vinca's lover was indeed called Alexis, but was not the philosophy teacher, and that he has therefore killed an innocent man.

SERIAL MURDERS

While looking through the school archives, Thomas also discovered a photo of Fanny (wearing a red wig) with Vinca during a play. The resemblance between the two girls is uncanny. Thomas tries to see Fanny, but first runs into her boyfriend, who informs him that Fanny has always been in love with him. Thomas confronts his former friend, who tells him that there are in fact two corpses buried in the ground: the second is that of Vinca, whom she herself had killed twenty-five years earlier.

When Thomas had left the feverish Vinca in Fanny's hands, Fanny, driven by jealousy, had prepared a cup of tea with a few Rohypnol tablets. A few hours later, back in Vinca's room, Fanny discovers that the young woman has consumed the tea and is no longer breathing. In shock, she faints and wakes up in the office of the school principal, Annabelle Degalais, Thomas' mother. She is told that she has two choices: confess to the murder and ruin her life or accept her help in hiding the body. She accepts and Francis buries Vinca's body alongside Alexis'. Annabelle puts on Alexis's cap and leaves for Paris by train with Fanny, wearing a red wig: they are the ones the witnesses have mistaken for

Alexis and Vinca, confirming the theory that they have fled in love.

But the few tablets Fanny slipped into the tea were not a lethal dose. The truth is discovered by Maxime, who learns that Vinca (after Fanny's departure) had tried to blackmail Annabelle by claiming to be pregnant by Richard. Furious, and not wanting her family life to be destroyed by the young girl, Annabelle had then grabbed a replica of a statue and smashed it on Vinca's skull, who died on the spot. Francis, Annabelle's lover, then took the body back to the girl's room, where it was dis-covered by Fanny. Fanny believes she has killed Vinca, so the lovers seize the opportunity and make her believe she is really guilty before burying the body.

However, during the high school ceremony, Maxime is pushed by a stranger and falls eight metres. While his friend is in hospital between life and death, Thomas goes to Francis' old house, where he discovers his affair with Annabelle and learns that he is his real father. He then receives a call from the police: his mother has just been found dead in Cap d'Antibes, killed with a rifle butt, and his father accuses Thomas of the murder.

A TRAGIC EPILOGUE

The next day, Thomas meets Corentin, Stéphane's trainee who has been investigating the financing of the gym: he learns that it was the Hutchinson & DeVille foundation that was behind it. Thomas then under-stands that Vinca loved women, and that her lover was the English literature professor, Alexis DeVille. She seeks to avenge Vinca's murder by killing those who were involved.

Thomas returns to Cap d'Antibes and is confronted by Alexis. She confesses that she learned about the double murder from Ahmed, whom she bribed with money. She loved Vinca madly, and pushed her to sleep with Richard in order to have a child with her. Thomas then accuses her of having perverted the teenager, notably by making her addicted to drugs. Alexis orders her dog to attack Thomas, but shots ring out: Richard has just shot the dog and Alexis, and saved his son's life.

Afterwards, Stéphane decides to bring the truth to light, even if it means sending his former friends to prison. During his further research, he discovers an article from 1997, mentioning acts of vandalism in the gym: it was a cover-up, orchestrated by Annabelle and Francis, that allowed them to evacuate the bodies.

With the disappearance of the bodies twenty years earlier saving him from prison, Thomas decides to write a novel based on the facts, but in which Vinca narrowly survives and disappears to start a new life elsewhere. "Somewhere, then, Vinca lived" (p. 423).

CHARACTER STUDY

THOMAS DEGALAIS

The novel's main narrator, Thomas Degalais, has been a writer since 2000. He has been living in the United States since 2000, but returns to France for his 50th high school anniversary, despite his aversion to such gatherings. Indeed, he has always been a great loner, with no real social ties ("You had no friends, Thomas. Your only friends were books," p. 183). He was very anxious by nature, and books brought him real peace. As a teenager, he had a "smart, preppy, clean-cut look, with his nice flannel jacket and sky-blue shirt" (p. 55) that he kept into adulthood. He was trained as a scientist, which he disliked, to please his parents, from whom he had now become considerably estranged – so much so that his mother had hidden from him the fact that she had had a heart attack a few months earlier. At the time, he considered Maxime his brother and Francis his father, as he was closer to them than to Richard: he was therefore not surprised to discover that Francis was his biological father and his mother's lover.

Throughout the novel, Thomas shows great determination and courage, especially when he confronts Alexis with her murders. This courage, surprising from a naturally anguished personality, is inspired by the love he had – and still has twenty-five years later – for Vinca.

Indeed, he has never felt anything like this for a woman since his teenage years.

VINCA ROCKWELL

Vinca is a complex girl, whom the reader only gets to know through the memories of the protagonists. She was "the girl all the boys were in love with" (p. 32), "atypical, cultured, lively and sparkling, with red hair, minnow eyes and fine features" (pp. 83-84). She was from the American bourgeoisie, the daughter of a French actress and an American Formula One driver, but orphaned in 1989. To Thomas, she was "the breed of lords" (p. 159), that is, "people who always had the leading roles in life, and when you were with them, relegated you directly to the status of an extra" (p. 159). This magnetic personality has fascinated people long after her death: not only did the girl stir up passions when her former classmates thought she was running away with her teacher, but in 2017, female students at the high school continue to worship her, creating a musical inspired by her last days and organising communication evenings in her old room at boarding school. But Vinca had a darker side. One day "glowing," the next she seemed "down or high" (p. 233). Addicted to drugs as a result of Alexis's bad influence, she also sought to take highly suggestive photographs in order to blackmail the Degalais couple.

MAXIME BIANCARDINI

The son of Francis, a masonry contractor, Maxime has always been more interested in blockbusters than literature. With an attractive physique, "sculpted torso, long surfer hair, Rip Curl shorts, laceless Vans" (p. 73), he has been friends with Thomas since childhood as they are neighbours, but the two men drift apart when Thomas moves to the US. He remains loyal to him, however, keeping his secret for twenty-five years.

Maxime is a homosexual and a family man: he had two daughters from a surrogate mother with Olivier, his partner. He is also running for a position as a Member of Parliament under the colours of President Emmanuel Macron's party, La République en marche.

STÉPHANE PIANELLI

A journalist at Nice-Matin, Stéphane is a member of the France Insoumise party and is politically committed. "With his long hair, musketeer's goatee, and round John Lennon-like glasses", this young man spent his entire school career in the same class as Thomas. He doesn't let himself be impressed by anyone and is determined to investigate, but above all to make a name for himself in investigative journalism. His ambition leads him to want to write a book that would send his former friends Thomas, Maxime and Fanny straight to prison. However, this plan falls through when he realises that the bodies have not been in the gym for twenty years.

FANNY BRAHIMI

A keen photographer, Thomas's former girlfriend studied medicine and now works as a cardiologist. As a teenager, she sported a *"grunge"* look (p. 51), but the "little blonde with light eyes and short hair" (p. 50) has mellowed as an adult.

She has been in love with Thomas since she was a teenager and has never stopped loving him. This one-sided love has led her to questionable actions: as a teenager, she had "started sleeping around without attaching herself to anyone" (p. 52) to heal her broken heart; she also made an attempt on Vinca's life by adding drugs to her tea; as an adult, she embarked on a serious relationship with Thierry without having feelings for him.

ANNABELLE DEGALAIS

Mother of Thomas and former headmistress of the Saint-Exupéry high school, Annabelle is above all a mother, ready to do anything to protect the balance of her family life: it is for this reason that this apparently simple and unremarkable woman kills Vinca in cold blood and convinces the young Fanny that she is responsible for the murder. It is to protect Thomas (despite their strained and distant relationship) that she finds Alexis DeVille, even if it means paying with her life. Francis' lifelong mistress, she has hidden the fact that he is Thomas' biological father for over four decades. However, she cannot help but feel an almost maternal tenderness for her lover's son, as well as for his children, acting almost like a grandmother in their presence.

RICHARD DEGALAIS

From the outset, Richard is presented as an unsympathetic person, capable of sleeping with a teenage girl simply because she tries to seduce him: "That little slut kept hanging around me. She turned me on and I cracked" (pp. 192-193). However, Richard is also loyal to his family, not hesitating to come to Thomas' rescue. Despite his affairs, he remains devoted to his wife, going mad with grief when he discovers her dead body at Cap d'Antibes.

KEYS TO READING

THE THRILLER/CRIME NOVEL GENRE

Features

With *La Jeune fille et la nuit*, Guillaume Musso confirms his status as a thriller author: he has become a "master of suspense" according to Cassandre Dupuis, literary critic for the newspaper Le Figaro. This is not an easy task: the thriller is a literary genre where it is difficult to renew and distinguish oneself, as it has been omnipresent for decades in literature, but also in the cinema and in other artistic and cultural media.

The thriller is an artistic genre that relies on suspense and tension that builds to a crescendo to keep the reader reading to find out more and to discover the outcome as quickly as possible. There are many twists and turns in thrillers, as in *The Girl and the Night* about the disappearance of Vinca: first thought to have run away with her teacher and lover, we then learn that the girl was killed by Fanny, only to discover that Annabelle was the real culprit.

The thriller genre is divided into multiple sub-genres, among which is the crime novel, which is characterized by six elements, all of which are present in *The Girl and the Night*:

- The crime (Vinca's disappearance);

- The motive (Annabelle's desire to protect her family from the young blackmailer);

- The culprit (Annabelle) and the victim (Vinca);

- The modus operandi (a statue smashed into the girl's skull);

- The investigation (led by Thomas for most of the novel).

As in traditional detective novels, the investigation, seemingly nebulous at first, gradually becomes clearer as the pages go by. The reader is led to make his or her own assumptions and to believe false leads (e.g. that Fanny was responsible for Vinca's death) before discovering the truth, which is frequently surprising and shocking. The twists and turns keep them reading until they get to the bottom of the investigation. The newspaper Le Soir referred to the novel as a "page-turner": this expression is often used to describe a book with breathtaking suspense, where it is difficult to stop reading until the end.

Musso's originality is expressed in the multiplicity of crimes: the original crime, the murder of Alexis by Thomas and Maxime; the second crime, the death of Vinca; the crimes of Alexis, who eliminated Francis and Annabelle and attempted to kill Maxime out of amorous revenge. Traditionally, the detective story focuses on a single mystery to be solved. However, the different plots of La Jeune fille et la nuit fit together perfectly: Vinca's murder is the reason for Alexis' murderous vendetta.

A Paragon of Paraliterature

Nevertheless, crime fiction is considered popular literature, aimed at a dilettante audience (as opposed to a more selective literary elite), because it sells millions of books each year. As such, this literary genre is part of paraliterature.

Theorist Marc Angenot defines paraliterature as "a vast domain of printed production excluded from the world of culture [...], a heterogeneous mass of objects [...] that seem to have nothing in common other than their alleged lack of aesthetic value" (Marc Angenot, *What is Paraliterature*, at www.erudit.org). As such, the detective novel was often decried by literary critics, who found it of no particular aesthetic interest, and therefore thought it unworthy. This is evidenced (at least until recently) by the absence of extensive literary studies on the subject.

Nevertheless, the detective novel (and more broadly the thriller genre – cinematographic or literary) has earned its credentials over the decades, and is now an essential genre in bookshops, where entire shelves are devoted to it. The same is true of the cinema and television, where crime films and series are multiplying in number and are becoming increasingly successful.

A PARTICULAR NARRATIVE STYLE: THE DOUBLE CHRONOLOGY

While the plot of *The Girl and the Night* takes place mainly in May 2017, entire chapters relate the events of December 1992. In both cases, the focus remains on Thomas, who remains the first-person narrator. There are, however, four notable exceptions through inserts at the end of some chapters, which reveal key elements of the plot: two sub-chapters are narrated directly by Annabelle (who recounts Vinca's murder as well as Alexis DeVille's threats), Fanny (who recounts her "murder" of Vinca), and Richard (who describes the moment he receives a letter from Annabelle after her disappearance, prompting him to protect Thomas and – ultimately – save him from Alexis' clutches).

Where most novels concentrate on a single focus throughout the plot, *The Girl and the Night* thus offers four interludes that enrich the novel by allowing for other narrative points of view.

The passages narrated by Thomas's parents are particularly interesting: while for most of the novel they are seen through the prism of their son, who has been distant for many years, these passages allow us to discover that both parents are in fact ready to make any sacrifice for him (death for Annabelle and prison for Richard). Moreover, their personalities are not really explored in depth at the beginning of the novel: Thomas mainly highlights the generational gap, dug since his adolescence by parents who pushed him into studies he did not like; the first-person narrative allows for a frank immersion in their feelings.

The narration from Fanny's point of view is also significant: it provides an initial answer to the mystery that Thomas is trying to solve (even if this will prove to be wrong in the subsequent events).

The double narrative of 1992 and 2017 helps to make the story more dynamic by breaking the traditional linear chronology of the detective novel. Moreover, the narrative inserts are narrated in the present tense, as if the protagonist were directly recounting his or her memories to someone (and in Fanny's case, to Thomas, to whom she is speaking directly). Conversely, the flashbacks from 1992 narrated by Thomas are in the past tense, as is the narrative of 2017. These flashbacks add a great deal to the narrative, as they allow access to the direct resolution of the mystery, unlike some novels where the denouement is explained simply through dialogue or long description.

THE THEME OF THE RELATIONSHIP: THOMAS AND VINCA

Until the publication of *The Girl and the Night*, Guillaume Musso was known for combining mystery and romance in more or less equal proportions in his works. This new novel marks a turning point in the themes addressed by the author, and the love story disappears from the foreground.

However, a love story emerges in the investigation: the relationship between Vinca and Thomas. This complex story seems to be a one-way street: the protagonists agree that Thomas was madly in love with Vinca, but the girl – it seems – never had any feelings for him. Even though the personalities of the two teenagers are opposite (Thomas is a great loner, while Vinca has a sunny personality that attracts many people), they share a common love of literature and have intense discussions about it.

As Fanny and Annabelle have repeatedly pointed out, Thomas was obsessed with Vinca, and nothing else mattered to him. To his mother's great despair, his school results even suffered. As an adult and a writer, Thomas publishes novels, in which – in Stéphane's eyes – Vinca is omnipresent. He is also willing to risk his life to find out what happened to the girl, as he seems to have a visceral need to solve the mystery.

Vinca, on the other hand, has no interest in Thomas, apart from their passion for literature. She only calls him when she needs him, and does not hesitate – for money – to put her friend's family in danger by sleeping with his father and then threatening his parents.

With the characters of Thomas and Vinca, Musso touches on the theme of unrequited love and the sometimes dramatic impact it can have.

AVENUES FOR REFLECTION

A FEW QUESTIONS FOR FURTHER REFLECTION...

* Which turn of events surprised you the most? For what reason(s)?

* Fanny reveals that she has been in love with Thomas since she was a teenager: did you spot any clues beforehand? If so, which ones?

* On page 161, Thomas asks: "Is Vinca a victim or an evil manipulator?" How would you answer this question?

* Based on your own readings of other novels by Guillaume Musso, how does *The Young Girl and the Night* differ from the author's previous novels?

* Among the former high school friends (Thomas, Maxime, Stéphane and Fanny), who do you feel closest to? Why or why not?

* Do you understand Thomas' obsession with Vinca?

* Does the relationship between Thomas and Vinca remind you of any other relationship (in literature, film or other artistic medium)?

* Do you think this complex plot could be adapted for film or television? What would be the possible difficulties?

TO GO FURTHER

REFERENCE EDITION

La Jeune Fille et la nuit, Paris, Calmann Levy, 2018, 424 p.

BENCHMARK STUDIES

Guillaume Musso tops the French novel sales charts for the seventh year, France TV Info, https://culturebox.francetvinfo.fr/livres/guillaume-musso-en-tete-des-ventes-de-romans-en-france-pour-la-septieme-annee-268137, 18 January 2018

GARY N., *Star de l'été, Guillaume Musso compte 1,2 million de lecteurs depuis janvier, ActuaLitté*, https://www.actualitte.com/article/monde-edition/star-de-l-ete-guillaume-musso-compte-1-2-million-de-lecteurs-depuis-janvier/90547, le 22 août 2018

Your opinion is important to us!
Leave a comment on the website of your online bookshop
and share your favourites on social networks!

Bright ≡Summaries.com

Although the editor makes every effort to verify the accuracy of the information published, BrightSummaries.com accepts no responsibility for the content of this book.

© BrightSummaries.com, 2023. All rights reserved.

www.brightsummaries.com

Ebook EAN: 9782808686624
Paperback EAN: 9782808698023
Legal Deposit: D/2023/12603/1082

Cover: © Primento
Digital conception by Primento, the digital partner of publishers.